GO TO SLEEP, JESSIE!

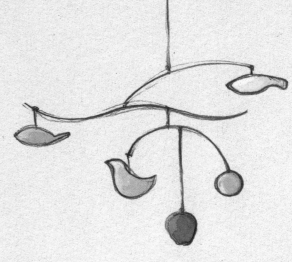

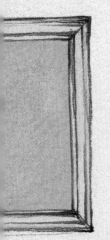

Little Hare Books
an imprint of
Hardie Grant Egmont
Ground Floor, Building 1, 658 Church Street
Richmond, Victoria 3121, Australia

www.littleharebooks.com

First published 2014
Reprinted 2015

This project has been assisted by the Australian Government through
the Australia Council for the Arts, its arts funding and advisory body.

Cataloguing-in-Publication details are available
from the National Library of Australia

978 1 742977 80 5 (hbk.)

Designed by Hannah Janzen
Produced by Pica Digital, Singapore
Printed through Asia Pacific Offset
Printed in Shenzhen, Guangdong Province, China

6 5 4 3 2

The illustrations in this book were created with watercolour, gouache and coloured pencil.

GO TO SLEEP, JESSIE!

LIBBY GLEESON & FREYA BLACKWOOD

LITTLE HARE
www.littleharebooks.com

FOR

JO
AND
JESS

—LG

Jessie is screaming.

Every night she does this.
Ever since she moved into my room.

'Be quiet,' I say. 'Go to sleep.'

She keeps screaming. She picks up her pillow and
tosses it out of the cot.

'You have to go to sleep,' I say.
'It's night-time.
Everything goes to sleep.'

Jessie keeps screaming.

'If you stop screaming,' I say,
'I'll let you hold T-Bear.'

I climb out of my bed and pass him to her.

Jessie holds him close.

For a moment all is quiet.

Then she tosses T-Bear
against the window. She opens
her mouth and screams.

I go downstairs.
Mum is reading a newspaper.

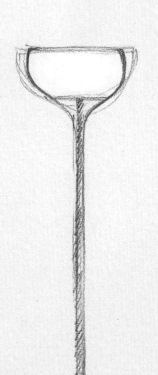

'She's keeping me awake,' I say.

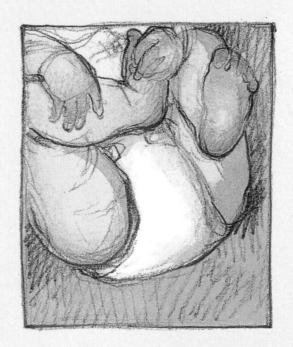

Mum comes up. She changes Jessie's nappy.
She pats Jess on the back and whispers a song.

I climb back into bed.

Mum tiptoes out of the room.

Jessie screams.

I go back downstairs.

Dad is watching television
and eating a chocolate.

'She's still keeping me awake.'

Dad comes up.

He tells Jess that all the birds
and pussy cats and puppy dogs are asleep.

He turns on her music box and
'This little piggy' fills the room.

He closes the door when he leaves.

Jessie screams.

I throw my blankets on the floor
and go downstairs.

'Can't you put her in your bed, Mum?'

Mum shakes her head.

'I want my own room back.'

'You wouldn't like that,' says Mum.

'I would so too.'

'Dad's going to put her
in the car and drive around
till she falls asleep.'

'Good.'

I stomp up the stairs.

It's quiet in our room.

I stand at the window and watch the car drive down
the street and turn around the corner.

Then it does it again and again.

I turn off the music and pick up T-Bear.

I climb into bed and pull the doona up to my chin.

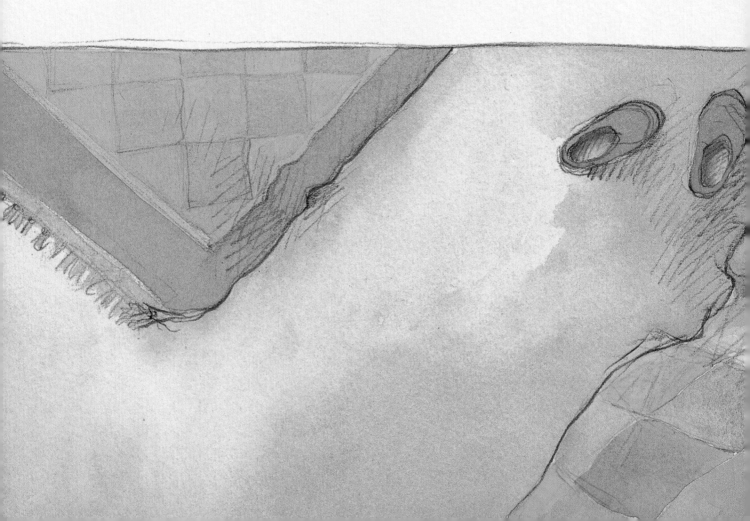

I can't sleep.

Dad comes in.

He puts Jessie down, covers her with her blanket
and creeps out of the room.

I watch her lying still.

She opens her eyes and stretches out her hands.

She grabs the bars of the cot and pulls herself up.

She stares at the closed door,
screws up her eyes
and screams.

I get out of bed and put my face up close to hers. Tears are running down her cheeks.

'Why don't you go to sleep?' I say.

I climb up over the bars of the cot and lie down.

Jessie stops crying. She stares at me for a moment
and then lies down beside me.

She giggles and puts her finger in my eye. 'Eye,' she says.

'Go to sleep.'

She sticks her finger up my nose. 'Nose,' she says.

'Sleep,' I say.

She snuggles up to me
and I put my arms around
her and hold her close.

She falls asleep.

I fall asleep too.